D1558625

Donna M. Fox

Jersey Girl

Copyright © 2015 Donna M. Fox, Jersey Girl Publications LLC
Written by Donna M. Fox
Illustrations by Sue Gioulis and Maria Lynskey
Graphic Design by KFR Communications

Printed by IngramSpark

ISBN-10: 0692555137
ISBN-13: 978-0-692555-13-2

Jersey Girl

An Illustrated Children's Book

Jersey Girl Publications

Dedicated to my loving family....

Thomas, Brad, Mom, Dad, and Daniel

Please visit www.jerseygirlpublications.com
to read about their influence on <u>Jersey Girl</u>.

Jersey Girl absolutely LOVES the summer!

The days are long, the nights are warm,

and the feeling is carefree.

Every morning, Jersey Girl wakes up and realizes it is a GIFT to be so close to the ocean.

She is THANKFUL.

On sunny days, time is brimming
with deep breaths of fresh air,
walks and talks,

neighbor visits and shopping,
boardwalk rides and games,
and of course BEACHTIME...

exploring at the ocean's edge,
finding unique shells, or just
staring in wonderment at the waves.

Even on a rainy day,
Jersey Girl is happy.

Her father would say, "A rainy day on vacation is better than a rainy day at home."

Jersey Girl puts on her flip flops
and rejoices in puddles, enjoys an
arcade with her brother, or cuddles
up with a good book on the couch.

Before sunset, Jersey Girl dances barefoot in her shore house kitchen to the music of Bruce and Bon Jovi as she joyfully helps prepare dinner.

The smell of barbecue, the feel of salt on her skin and sand between her toes, and anticipation of her nightly bike ride...

...cozy in a sweatshirt,
inhaling that beautiful salt air,
with the one-of-a-kind taste of
Milky Way ice cream on the boardwalk
at dusk...

...leads her to fall asleep
peacefully with the porch doors open
and remnants of all of those dreamy
summer scents drifting in.

Down the shore
everything's all right.

Share your memories.

Use this space to write or illustrate your own
special Jersey Shore or beach vacation story.

About Us

Illustrator

A resident of Ocean Grove, NJ, Sue Gioulis is an artist whose talents are displayed in the illustrations of several children's books as well as in the Main Avenue Galleria in Ocean Grove. She received her formal training at the Ringling College of Art and Design and is a member of the Manasquan River Group of Artists.

Author

Born and raised in NJ, Donna Fox is a special education teacher of 17 years with a specialty in language arts who stepped away from her love of teaching to raise her son with all of that love. Donna's fond memories of the Jersey Shore combined with her favorite pastime of reading to her son inspired her to write Jersey Girl, a joyful combination of past and present.

Illustrator

The mother of Donna, Maria Lynskey has been sketching, painting, and involved with the arts since she was a child. Great family memories at the Jersey Shore were captured by her on film in the 1970s and were the catalyst for many pages of this book. Her beautiful oil paintings are cherished contributions to Jersey Girl as well.

CPSIA information can be obtained
at www.ICGtesting.com
Printed in the USA
BVOW10*1806160316

440300BV00009B/4/P